What Kids Say About
Carole Marsh Mysteries . . .

"I love the real locations! Reading the book always makes me want to go and visit them all on our next family vacation. My mom says maybe, but I can't wait!"

"One day, I want to be a real kid in one of Ms. Marsh's mystery books. I think it would be fun, and I think I am a real character anyway. I filled out the application and sent it in and am keeping my fingers crossed!"

"History was not my favorite subject until I started reading Carole Marsh Mysteries. Ms. Marsh really brings history to life. Also, she leaves room for the scary and fun."

"I think Christina is so smart and brave. She is lucky to be in the mystery books because she gets to go to a lot of places. I always wonder just how much of the book is true and what is made up. Trying to figure that out is fun!"

"Grant is cool and funny! He makes me laugh a lot!"

"I like that there are boys and girls of different ages in the story. Some mysteries I outgrow, but I can always find a favorite character to identify with in these books."

"They are scary, but not too scary. They are funny. I learn a lot. There is always food which makes me hungry. I feel like I am there."

What Parents and Teachers Say about Carole Marsh Mysteries . . .

"I think kids love these books because they have such a wealth of detail. I know I learn a lot reading them! It's an engaging way to look at the history of any place or event. I always say I'm only going to read one chapter to the kids, but that never happens–it's always two or three, at least!"
–Librarian

"Reading the mystery and going on the field trip–Scavenger Hunt in hand–was the most fun our class ever had! It really brought the place and its history to life. They loved the real kids characters and all the humor. I loved seeing them learn that reading is an experience to enjoy!"
–4th grade teacher

"Carole Marsh is really on to something with these unique mysteries. They are so clever; kids want to read them all. The Teacher's Guides are chock full of activities, recipes, and additional fascinating information. My kids thought I was an expert on the subject–and with this tool, I felt like it!"
–3rd grade teacher

"My students loved writing their own Real Kids/Real Places mystery book! Ms. Marsh's reproducible guidelines are a real jewel. They learned about copyright and more and ended up with their own book they were so proud of!"
–Reading/Writing Teacher

"The kids seem very realistic–my children seemed to relate to the characters. Also, it is educational by expanding their knowledge about the famous places in the books."

"They are what children like: mysteries and adventures with children they can relate to."

"Encourages reading for pleasure."

"This series is great. It can be used for reluctant readers, and as a history supplement."

The COLONIAL CAPER Mystery at WILLIAMSBURG

by
Carole Marsh

Published by Gallopade International/Carole Marsh Books. Printed in the United States of
America.

Managing Editor: Sherry Moss
Senior Editor: Janice Baker
Assistant Editor: Susan Walworth
Cover Design: Yvonne Ford
Cover Photo Credits: Courtesy, The Colonial Williamsburg Foundation
Picture Credits: Lori J. White
Content Design and Illustrations: Yvonne Ford

Gallopade International is introducing SAT words that kids need to know in each
new book that we publish. The SAT words are bold in the story. Look for this
special logo beside each word in the glossary. Happy Learning!

Gallopade is proud to be a member and supporter of these educational organizations and
associations:

American Booksellers Association
American Library Association
International Reading Association
National Association for Gifted Children
The National School Supply and Equipment Association
The National Council for the Social Studies
Museum Store Association
Association of Partners for Public Lands
Association of Booksellers for Children
Association for the Study of African American Life and History
National Alliance of Black School Educators

30 YEARS AGO . . .

As a mother and an author, one of the fondest periods of my life was when I decided to write mystery books for children. At this time (1979), kids were pretty much glued to the TV, something parents and teachers complained about the way they do about video games today.

I decided to set each mystery in a real place—a place kids could go and visit for themselves after reading the book. And I also used real children as characters. Usually a couple of my own children served as characters, and I had no trouble recruiting kids from the book's location to also be characters.

Also, I wanted all the kids—boys and girls of all ages—to participate in solving the mystery. And, I wanted kids to learn something as they read. Something about the history of the location. And I wanted the stories to be funny.

That formula of real+scary+smart+fun served me well. The kids and I had a great time visiting each site, and many of the events in the stories actually came out of our experiences there.

I love getting letters from teachers and parents who say they read the book with their class or child, then visited the historic site and saw all the places in the mystery for themselves. What's so great about that? What's great is that you and your children have an experience that bonds you together forever. Something you shared. Something you both cared about at the time. Something that crossed all age levels—a good story, a good scare, a good laugh!

30 years later,

Carole Marsh

Hey, kids! As you see—here we are ready to embark on another of our exciting Carole Marsh Mystery adventures! You know, in "real life," I keep very close tabs on Christina, Grant, and their friends when we travel. However, in the mystery books, they always seem to slip away from Papa and I so that they can try to solve the mystery on their own!

I hope you will go to www.carolemarshmysteries.com and apply to be a character in a future mystery book! Well, The *Mystery Girl* is all tuned up and ready for "take-off!"

Gotta go... Papa says so! Wonder what I've forgotten this time?

Happy "Armchair Travel" Reading,

Mimi

Christina Yother **Grant Yother** **Josh Tolin** **Francesca Vranesevich**

A BOUT THE CHARACTERS

Christina Yother, 10, from Peachtree City, Georgia

Grant Yother, 7, from Peachtree City, Georgia, Christina's brother

Josh Tolin, 10, from Peachtree City, Georgia, as William

Francesca Vranesevich, 9, from Peachtree City, Georgia, as Mary

The many places featured in the book actually exist and are worth a visit! Perhaps you could read the book and follow the trail these kids went on during their mysterious adventure!

TITLES IN THE CAROLE MARSH MYSTERIES SERIES

Books and Teacher's Guides are available at booksellers, libraries, school supply stores, museums, and many other locations!

CONTENTS

PROLOGUE

On a foggy autumn night, with golden-hued leaves pasted in a paisley pattern across a dirt road, a man wearing a wig white as snow, descended from a horse-drawn carriage.

He might have been George Washington... Thomas Jefferson...or Patrick Henry, but he wasn't. His name was never known. Indeed, save the evidence you are about to hear, there is no reason to believe that he ever passed through the ghostly, fogged-in village.

The village was, like all of America at that time, still ruled by England. As clouds scattered and the full moon peered out, the British Union Jack snapped sharp in the brisk breeze.

This village of Williamsburg, by daylight, a bustling, prosperous, British colony in Virginia, now slept. No one ever saw the bewigged man stomp through the leaves to a large oak tree. As if by pre-plan and design, he tugged at a knothole and removed the wooden plug. Into the space, he placed an object and replaced the plug to stopper the hole tightly.

He returned to the carriage, to attend a ball? A funeral? An urgent mission of state? No one ever knew. *The carriage sped off into the night.* *The tree grew taller over the years.* *The knothole kept the secret.*

1 THE ROYAL COLONY

"We're doomed!" said Grant.

Christina, trying to finish her math homework in one of the back seats of the *Mystery Girl*, nodded in agreement. "You know Mimi won't let us take off without the pre-flight lecture, little brother. She always traps us like this! While Papa fuels the plane, we're her captives. Uh-oh, here she comes—get ready!"

Grant groaned and swiped his forehead. He sat in the pilot's seat while his grandfather held the fuel hose and grinned up at his grandson. Even he knew what their grandmother was about to do.

Sure enough, the airplane door flew open and Mimi, wearing her usual red suit and heels, popped into the other front seat of the airplane, tugging her ever-present tote bag of history research behind her.

1

As soon as she was settled, she blew kisses to her grandkids and began. "Now you know," she said, "we just can't leave Falcon Field here in Peachtree City and head for Virginia without me giving you some background, right?"

As she pulled a book out of her tote bag, she ignored Grant's groan but smiled when Christina slammed her math notebook closed and snapped to attention.

"Hurry, Papa, save us!" Grant squealed out the window.

"Now, Grant," said Mimi, "be still. You'll want to hear this! As you know, we're headed to Williamsburg in eastern Virginia. It was the former capital of the royal colony, before America was America."

"I thought Jamestown was the capital," said Christina.

"It was the first capital," Mimi explained. "But when the statehouse there burned, it was decided to move the capital to a new town. Williamsburg was named in honor of British King William III."

"And we care about all this—why?" groused Grant, leaning his head forward on the plane's steering wheel.

Mimi, who wrote mystery books filled with flabbergasting history for kids, looked appalled. "Why, because it's HISTORY! Our history. America's history!"

Grant still looked dissatisfied and thrust his head harder against the wheel. "But will there be a test?" he asked, unhappily.

Mimi sat back, relaxed, in her seat. She had a serious look on her usually smiling face. "Oh, Grant," she said, "when it comes to history, there's always a test. Many tests. And the outcome makes all the difference."

Christina knew her grandmother didn't mean a school test. She was just about to ask her what she did mean, when she felt a strange sensation. Suddenly, she reached across the front seat and grabbed her brother.

"Grant! Grant! Sit up!" she cried.

"THE PLANE IS MOVING!!"

2 Uncle Wig and Aunt Halfpenney

"Stop! Stop!" shouted Christina and Mimi. Grant looked dumbfounded; what had he done, he wondered.

As his family went a little bonkers in the cockpit, Papa (called the Cowboy Pilot by Mimi), just whipped out the rope he always carried and lassoed the left strut of the barely moving airplane. "Got it!" he shouted up to them.

In a second, he had retrieved his rope, slapped his cowboy hat on his head, and hopped into the plane. Grant had already scurried to the back seat beside his sister, figuring he was in Big Trouble.

But his grandfather just grinned. "You gotta take flying lessons before you can fly, little buddy," he said with a wink.

Mimi fanned herself mightily with a travel brochure. "Oh my goodness! We're supposed to be going on an adventure, not having one right here on the tarmac even before we leave!"

Grant slunk lower in the backseat. To help her brother out and change the subject, Christina asked, "Can you tell us more about Williamsburg, please?" Grant gave his sister a "What are you thinking!" look.

Mimi sighed. "Oh, not right now," she said. "I'm too shook up. Maybe later, ok?"

In spite of themselves, Papa, Christina, and especially Grant, all laughed.

"Uh, ok, sure, Mimi," Grant finally said, trying to sound disappointed but failing miserably since he was spurting giggle spit at the same time. "We'll wait." And under his breath muttered, "*Forever*."

Fortunately, the rest of the flight was uneventful. Everyone was mesmerized by the bright October sky, the counterpane quilt of colorful trees below, and the glint of ribbon rivers like silver thread in the sun. When the village of Colonial Williamsburg came into view, Christina gasped.

"Oh, Mimi!" she said. "It's beautiful— especially with the autumn colors. It looks just like a little pretend village."

Her grandmother nodded her blond curls toward the window. "Colonial Williamsburg is certainly one of the most beautiful historic sites in America. Tourists actually get to walk where history was constantly being made. America was just a baby back then!"

"History schmystery," grumbled Grant, waking up and stretching. "History's a mystery to me."

"No one said anything about mystery," Mimi insisted. "This is just a simple, quick, ordinary research trip. A quick tour. Some good colonial food. A little shopping..."

"Buying a million books..." Papa interrupted, banking the plane toward the final approach to the runway.

"Buying a million books..." Mimi agreed with a grin.

In the back, Christina and Grant cackled.

"What's so funny?" their grandmother demanded.

"You, Mimi!" said Christina. "You said no mystery. Where you go there's always a mystery!"

And sure enough, by the time they landed the plane, unloaded their luggage, caught a taxi into town, and got out in front of a colonial house, mystery was afoot!

"Welcome!" squealed Uncle Wig, adjusting his white powdered wig, which shifted nervously around his bald head.

"Get in here!" cried Aunt Halfpenny, shaking her white apron. "There's a mystery to solve and no time to lose!"

3 MYSTERY AFOOT!

Inside the quaint, snug, and cozy colonial cottage, the families hugged. Uncle Wig and Aunt Halfpenny weren't really their relatives. Mimi had met them on a previous research trip when she stayed in their upstairs guest bedroom. They hit it off so well, that the older couple just insisted their home be their first stop in Colonial Williamsburg.

Uncle Wig and Aunt Halfpenny were long-time interpreters in the historic district. They dressed and spoke as if they lived in Colonial Williamsburg long ago.

"What's going on?" asked Mimi, sorry to see her friends so agitated.

Aunt Halfpenny plopped down into an overstuffed chair. "A very important map has been stolen."

"Uh," said Grant. "I can go down to the welcome center and get you another map of Virginia."

"Thanks, Grant," said Uncle Wig, patting Grant's head. "But this is a priceless map. It shows the royal colony of Virginia in 1750. That's when Virginia included land that went west as far as the Mississippi River and north as far as the Great Lakes."

"Wow!" said Christina. "I didn't know that. But what's so special about that map?"

Aunt Halfpenny sighed so hard that Mimi put her hand on the old woman's shoulder. "There's a big event in Colonial Williamsburg on Saturday night. A ball! The map is to be presented as a special gift."

"To whom?" Mimi asked.

Together, Aunt Halfpenny and Uncle Wig— with bug eyes—announced loudly:

"THE QUEEN OF ENGLAND!"

Soon, both families were situated at a table at Christiana Campbell's Tavern, a popular eating establishment, still talking about the just-learned mystery.

"You have to remember," said Papa, as they waited for their food to come, "that when Virginia was a British colony, they were supposed to make money for the Crown. Tobacco was a very important crop. Farms surrounded the village here. People grew tobacco and other crops and sent them back to England. Since Williamsburg was the capital city, it was doubly busy with visitors, lawmakers, and other people from near and far."

"Then what happened?" Christina asked.

Uncle Wig, still tugging at his snow-colored headpiece, took up the story. "Oh, the colonists got aggravated at having to pay higher and higher taxes to England. They decided they wanted to rule themselves and control their own destiny. Some of the people you heard debating those issues here were Thomas Jefferson,

Patrick Henry, and other famous patriots of the day, like George Washington!"

"So that's when we had the War for Independence?" asked Grant.

"Very good, Grant," said Mimi, proudly. "Yes, and later the capital of Virginia was moved to Richmond."

"But it looks so real!" said Christina. "It's hard to believe that now it's just a living museum. I feel like I've been transported back in time!"

"I feel like a starving colonist!" Grant said, and on cue his tummy rumbled loudly.

Also, as if on cue, waitresses in ruffled aprons and caps appeared and spread before them an amazing array of yummy-looking 18th century food:

Lump crab cakes

Gloucester chicken

Clam stew

OYSTER SALET

Fried hen

Mushroom ragout

Pickled watermelon

Spiced sweet potatoes

Molly?s macaroni

"What a feast!" said Papa, who was always hungry and loved good food.

"They really knew how to cook back then," agreed Mimi, taking a deep breath at all the wonderful aromas.

"Why do they spell things funny on the menu?" asked Grant. "Like *salet* for salad."

"I know that!" said Christina, her mouth watering. "Spelling came over from England and back then even a simple word like spelling could be *speled* different ways. It wasn't until we got dictionaries that spelling was more standardized."

"Well, those colonists wouldn't have passed my spelling tests at school!" said Grant, chomping down onto a fat chicken drumstick.

"Please tell us more about the missing map," Christina suggested, as they all began to fill their plates and eat. "Maybe we can help." She ignored her grandmother's frown.

"Ohhhh," said Aunt Halfpenny, who was so upset that she seemed to have no appetite. She nibbled on a corn muffin and said, "The map is just beautiful and very historic and priceless, as I said. It had been hanging in one of the buildings in Colonial Williamsburg, but had been sent out for restoration before being presented to the Queen. When someone went to pick it up, it had vanished!"

"Now, now," said Uncle Wig, patting his wife's plump hand. "There's not a thing we can do about it. Perhaps it's just misplaced. It will show up by Saturday, I'm sure."

Silence all around the table indicated that he was the only one who thought so.

As the meal was finished, Papa said, "Well, I have an airplane to maintain."

"And I have an appointment with a curator," Mimi said, glancing at her watch.

Aunt Halfpenny wiped her mouth primly with her white cloth napkin. "I have to get back to my post welcoming the visitors."

"And I must return to the wig shop," said Uncle Wig, swiping yet again at his crooked wig cap.

Christina and Grant gave each other one of their secret looks that pretty much translated as "Well, we don't have anything to do but solve this mystery!"

But before anyone could move, dessert was

placed before them. Mystery would just have to
wait a few more minutes for:

> *Cream pie with chocolate shavings*
> *Cherry pie with ice cream*
> *Lemon chess pie with sweet cream*

"Yum yum!" cried Christina.

"YUM!" SAiD MiMi.

"Yummy mummy in my tummy," said Grant.

"I think I may need a nap after this!"
said Papa.

Only Uncle Wig and Aunt Halfpenny made no
comment about the scrumptious-looking
desserts. They both seemed lost in thought,
sad, worried, and, well, about to cry.

However, unnoticed by them all, a man in the

colonial costume of a very important looking person, sat nearby, also finishing his meal. He was alone. He stared at them. And he looked very, very angry. He tapped his buckled shoe impatiently on the wooden floor. And when they left...he followed them.

4 WALKABOUT IN WILLIAMSBURG

As they left Christiana Campbell's Tavern, Christina and Grant were delighted to hear the following conversation:

Mimi: "I've got to be off to my appointment."

Aunt Halfpenny: "I've got to hurry to work!"

Uncle Wig: "Me, too; I'm almost late!"

Papa: "I've got to go and secure the *Mystery Girl* for the night!"

All four adults stared at the children, then at one another.

Aunt Halfpenny said: "It really is safe here in Colonial Williamsburg, if the children would like to take a tour on their own."

Mimi: "Well, I'm not sure."

Papa: "Aw, they'll be fine."

Uncle Wig: "I'll give them the key to our cottage. They can walk back and meet you there later."

Soon it was agreed and Uncle Wig pulled a large skeleton key from his pocket and gave it to Grant. The kids promised that they'd be careful. Mimi gave Christina her cell phone and said, "Now call me on Papa's cell phone if you need anything!" She took Papa's cell phone from his shirt pocket. "Promise?"

"PROMISE!"

screeched the two children. They loved to explore on their own, and this was their chance.

The adults waved and went their ways, while Christina and Grant just stood there and grinned.

"What first?" asked Grant.

"Not sure," said his sister. "Let's just walk down the main street and see what's going on. We can get back to the house in a little while—no rush."

Without another word, the children hopped off the tavern steps and headed down the Duke of Gloucester Street—off on adventure, and, of course, in search of the missing map!

It was a warm fall afternoon and, as it turned out, the kids were not in as big a hurry to solve the mystery, as they were to take in all the amazing sights and sounds.

They both felt as if it were 200 years ago. History was in the air! As they strolled around, they encountered visitors like themselves, but also, so many people dressed in period costume, that it just seemed as if the past had come to life!

Market Square was filled with open-air stands overrun with colorful fall crops like pumpkins, squash, Indian corn, gourds, and more. Servants from the fine houses haggled with farmers over the price of chickens and cabbages before finally shrugging and making their purchases.

"Hey, Christina, let's buy Mimi a gourd!"

Christina looked at her brother like he was crazy. "What in the world for?"

"I think she would like it," Grant said. "Plus, I'd like to try this haggling over price thing—I think I'd be good at it."

Christina shook her head. "Knock yourself out, little brother. Go get in the buying fray. And good luck!"

Excitedly, Grant waded into the throng of buyers and sellers. His sister watched him bargain over a large green and yellow striped gourd. There was a lot of head shaking back and forth, and then, finally, a lot of headshaking up and down, then a handshake. Grant ran back to her holding what Christina thought was the ugliest thing she had ever seen, especially its long, curved neck.

But she sure didn't want to rain on Grant's parade, as the saying went.

"Look!" Grant shouted, holding up the gourd with one hand. "At first, the farmer said no because I only had these..." With his other hand, he pulled out some dollar bills. "But then I remembered Uncle Wig had given me these..." Changing hands, he plucked a handful of colonial coins out of his other pocket. "I got a gourd and change!" he said proudly.

"Good job!" Christina bragged. "You also have a few chicken feathers stuck to the back of your pants!" Giggling, she spun Grant around and plucked his "tailfeathers."

"Hey, what are you doing back there?" Grant grumbled.

He spun around to see his sister looking quite puzzled. "What's that?" he asked.

A "rear-ended" clue!

Christina held up a modern-day sticky note that was stuck to her brother's hindquarters. "That's a very good question," his sister answered in a low voice. "To me, it sounds like...a

5 AND SO IT BEGINS...

Grant read the note aloud:

> You don't really belong here.
> Perhaps you should
> go back home.
> The thing you seek
> belongs to me.
> It's <u>mine</u> and <u>mine</u> alone!

Grant hugged the gourd to his chest. "This is for Mimi!" he said, angrily. "It's mine. I bought it fair and square."

Christina folded the note and put it in her pocket. "I don't think whoever wrote this means your gourd, Grant," she said. "I think they mean the missing map. At least I think that's what I think."

Grant laughed. "You're out of your gourd, Christina," he said. "We've hardly been in Colonial Williamsburg anytime. Who even knows about the missing map? And who could possibly know that we made a pact to find it?"

Christina scuffed the toe of her shoe in the dry dirt roadway. She looked all around at the visitors dressed in modern-day attire, as well as the endless number of colonial-era farmers, Native Americans, aristocrats, and others going to and fro about their business.

Why hadn't they paid more attention, she wondered. She and Grant knew the mystery drill. It always started early, just almost as soon as they and Mimi and Papa got somewhere. How did that always happen? Mimi and Papa always got busy. She and Grant always committed to solve the mystery and save the day. But usually, they had their mystery-solving antennae up early. How could she have been so lax?

"What is it?" asked Grant. "What's wrong?"

"Well," said Christina, "it's clear that the only person who could possibly have overheard us discuss the missing map and our resolve to find it was eating at Christiana Campbell's Tavern at the same time we were. Only we weren't really paying attention to the people around us. So I have no clue who could be on to us already—on to us enough to already leave us a threatening clue."

Grant hoisted the gourd up to his chest. "Aw, don't worry," he said. "Besides, we are good at this mystery-solving, don't you think? They're not on to us...we are on to them!"

Christina frowned. "Look around, Grant," she insisted. "On to who, or whom, or whomever, whichever way you say it?"

Slowly, Grant did a 360-degree turn. In every direction he saw people and more people. Frontiersmen. Jugglers. Soldiers. Planters. Farmers. Men. Women. Children. "Uh, I think I see what you mean," he admitted. "The person who overhead us could be anyone, right?"

His sister nodded. "Any one of the about 1,800 people Aunt Halfpenny said lived in Williamsburg...or any of the hundreds of daily visitors...not to mention the official workers all dressed like the..."

"It could be anyone!" Grant whispered loudly. "But really, I think it's just HIM!" He pointed across the road to a man dressed all in black as if he were an old-timey preacher or something.

Christina stared. "And why do you think it's him?"

Grant grinned. "Look at what he's holding! A pack of sticky notes. And just how many colonial gentlemen do you know who were the proud owners of 20th century sticky notes back in that day? I told you we were pretty good at this mystery-solving thing!"

Quickly, Christina turned she and her brother away from the man before he could see them. "I think you're right, Grant! And so it begins! Mystery's afoot and it looks like it wears belt-buckle shoes. We got lucky this time, didn't we? Now, let's slowly turn around and follow him instead of him following us. Slowly now," she warned.

But when they turned, the man was gone. Oh, yes, they had the right man. They thought they had lost him, but he had not lost them. He was very good at what he did too, and it most certainly did not involve nosy, little, pesky, stubborn tourist kids. He waited until they finally turned away and headed down Duke of Gloucester Street and began to follow them. The sooner he found out where they were staying, the sooner he could be rid of them!

6 THE KING'S ARMS

Soon, in spite of their consternation over the curious note and their disappointment at losing sight of the man, Christina and Grant once more found themselves eagerly pretending to be colonial kids of the past.

It was not hard to imagine! As they walked, they spotted stores filled with imported chocolate, coffee, and tea. Large sacks of corn and flour were heaped upon a wooden cart being pulled by a plantation slave of the past.

Colonial gardens still sprouted colorful flowers behind white picket fences. The smell of roasting oysters wafted through the autumn air. A small boy hawked *The Virginia Gazette* to passersby.

Men in white wigs, tricorn hats, white stockings and belt-buckle shoes jostled one another in the busy streets. Their long coats flew open in their hurry, exposing brocade vests. Some of the men traveled on foot; others clopped by in horse drawn carriages. All looked important, earnest, and determined.

"What's going on?" Grant asked. "Seems like all these old guys with bad hair days are headed someplace."

One of the men breezed by Grant and stopped right in front of him. He tapped his walking stick on the ground. "Why, we're headed to a session of the General Assembly, young man!" he nearly shouted at Grant. "It meets here in the Capitol today! You should come along and watch the proceedings! Most impressive! Most impressive!" Without waiting for a reply, the man hurried off.

Christina laughed. "Well, I guess that answered your question, Grant! Maybe we should take him up on his offer. After that big lunch, I'd be glad to just sit around for awhile."

"And watch a bunch of old men talk?" Grant groused. "I don't think so!"

But Christina was already headed in the direction of the Capitol. "They're not just talking, they're arguing and debating and making laws and making HISTORY!"

When Grant still hung back, Christina bent down and whispered, "Besides, if we are looking for a man in a white wig and a black suit, well, that seems like the place he might be headed as well?"

That got Grant's interest. "Ok," he agreed, "but if he is not there, I'm leaving. It's too pretty a day to be stuck in some dumb, old building. Besides, I'd rather look for the map than the man."

But Grant found that he was talking to himself, for his sister had scampered on ahead and he had to run to catch up.

The Capitol building was a handsome brick structure at the east end of Duke of Gloucester Street. Its rounded sides made it look a bit jolly. Otherwise, it was in the traditional H-shape that meant the royal governor and his council were in a separate, swanky, "upper house" wing from the plain wing of the "lower house" of burgesses.

A costumed interpreter outside told a tour group, "Patrick Henry gave his famous speech against the Stamp Act here. On any given day, you might also see George Washington, George Mason, Thomas Jefferson, and other famous men of the Revolution!"

"Well, we just want to see one guy," Grant said, as they passed through the doors.

"Shhh..." warned Christina as they entered the building. Someone directed them to the historical drama in progress, which was a trial in the General Court.

Serious-looking men sat in a semi-circle against dark paneling. A glistening chandelier hung overhead. An interpreter silently directed them to a seat. As soon as they sat down, both Christina and Grant realized the same thing— what appeared to be the chief judge in the proceedings was the man they were hunting.

"This can't be good," whispered Christina to her brother.

"What if he sees us?" Grant whispered back, his voice with a tremor.

But it was too late! The man in black suddenly stood up and swung his gavel hard with

a GIANT BANG!

With a long, bony finger he pointed directly at the two children.

"This court is adjourned!" he cried. "And I will see YOU in The King's Arms!"

And then he really stunned them by turning and saying, "Bailiff, take these two youngsters to The King's Arms immediately!"

And off, Christina and Grant were whisked!

7 A BUG IN HIS EAR

As the bailiff briskly escorted the two embarrassed children out of the Capitol and down the street, Grant asked his sister, "Are we really going to be thrown into the king's arms? That sounds dangerous!"

Before Christina could answer, the bailiff gave a gruff laugh. "The King's Arms is no place for tomfoolery," he barked.

Christina and Grant gave each other a nervous look. They did not know what 'tomfoolery' was, but it sounded like they were in trouble!

But before they could argue, or pull away, the bailiff whisked them into a building with a fancy crest on the front that said,

THE KING'S ARMS

As soon as they were inside, they realized that it was just another tavern!

"Uh, we've already eaten, thank you," Grant protested, as they were brusquely escorted to a seat at a table.

"Really!" Christina insisted. "We can't stay. Our grandparents are expecting us."

The bailiff just ignored the children, got them settled, hailed a waitress, and ordered "Two peanut soups and two Norfolk pottage pyes."

Just as quickly as the bailiff disappeared, the strange judge showed up, and took a seat in front of them. He surprised them both by giving them a big grin!

"Well, hello!" he said. "How do you like the genteel King's Arms tavern? There are a lot of taverns here outside the Capitol to serve the hungry and thirsty."

When Christina and Grant just stared at him in awe, he added, "Let me introduce myself. I'm George, your Uncle Wig's brother. He saw me at Christiana Campbell's and put a bug in my ear to keep an eye on you two."

Christina almost giggled when she saw her brother straining to see if the man really had a bug in his ear. "We thought..." she began. "That is, we thought..."

George laughed. "That I was the map thief? That's what Uncle Wig was worried about. Your reputation precedes you! He and your Papa thought it best you be diverted from trying to find the missing map."

"But it's important!" said Christina, aggravated and feeling tricked. "Someone has to look for it! Mimi says it would be just terrible for the Queen to come all the way from England to receive an empty frame."

Once more, George laughed. "I'm sure she just meant that as a figure of speech. Many people are on the lookout for the map," he assured them. "They don't need help from a couple of tourist kids."

"Have they found it?" Grant asked softly.

Now George looked flustered. "Well, no, no, not that I've heard, but it's just a matter of time."

"But what about the note with the threat on it?" Christina said. "Why did you give us that? I don't think Papa would think that was funny at all."

It was clear from the look on his face that George had no idea about the note, or clue, as Grant and Christina now thought of it.

"What note?" he asked.

Christina and Grant gave each other their secret mystery look that meant "Don't tell."

Quickly, Grant began to scrap his pewter spoon through his bowl. "Boy, this peanut soup is really, really good!"

Christina was suddenly very hungry too and began to gobble her pottage pye.

George just shook his head and muttered, "What curious children..."

After their second lunch, Christina and Grant headed for Uncle Wig's and Aunt Halfpenny's house with directions from George, who had to return to his duties at the Capitol in time for the next tour.

"So where did that note come from, Christina?" Grant asked as they wandered, full and tired, down the now less busy street.

"Maybe it wasn't for us at all," pondered Christina. "But I don't think we should give up map-hunting just because of a false alarm with this George guy, do you?"

Her brother looked perplexed. "There was a false alarm? I didn't hear it."

"Oh, Grant," Christina said. "That's just a figure of speech!"

"Everyone with their colonial talk and weird spelling and figures of speech, why it gives me, it gives me, a bug in my ear!" Grant complained, but his sister only giggled.

Aggravated, Grant stomped ahead of her. That was when she saw the note stuck to the back of her brother's shirt.

"What's this?" she asked, pulling it off.

Grant turned on his heel. "What?! Ohhh... not another one?"

"Looks like," Christina said, glancing around. Who was getting so close to them they could attach a note?

"Let me see," said Grant, snatching the note away from her and reading aloud:

Oh, curious children
Funny ye be;
You make me want to
Slap my knee
And wonder when
You'll find the map
Is not your friend!

"What's that funny thing?" Christina asked, her finger tracing the image. "It seems familiar, sort of."

"I don't know, but a lot of the shops around here have funny-looking signs over them. Maybe it's one of those," said Grant.

As they walked on, they stopped at each shop to check the signs overhead.

"Why don't the shops just have names?" asked Grant.

"Maybe all the people couldn't read?" Christina guessed. "Besides, this is more fun! It's like a puzzle, trying to figure out what each shop is."

Always lovers of games and puzzles and riddles, Christina and Grant had soon turned looking for the "funny" sign into a game. They tried to see who could guess the most sign meanings correctly.

[Reader, try your hand at the game on the next page, then we'll get back to the story! The correct answers can be found at the end of this book. You can go to www.carolemarshmysteries.com, and print out this activity so you can write your answers! Do not write in this book!]

Match the Sign with the Shop!

1. Milliner
2. Apothecary
3. Tailor
4. Blacksmith
5. Barber
6. Shoemaker
7. Gunsmith
8. Brickmaker
9. Wheelwright
10. Saddler
11. Silversmith
12. Carpenter

Answers on page 135.

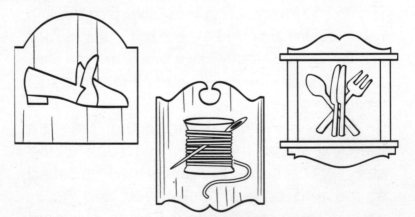

"Well, you got more than me," Grant grumbled. "But why can't we figure this weird sign out? It's the one we need."

The afternoon was waning on and Christina and Grant were getting tired. The tourists were clearing out as the evening grew cooler. Shadows followed them down a lane. So did a small boy.

He, too, was in costume. And he shocked Christina when he suddenly tugged at her jacket. She spun around.

"Hey, what..." she began.

"Sorry, mum," said the small boy, doffing a cap. "Just overheard you and your brother talking about that sign." He pointed to the image on the note they held. "It's for the printer and bookbinder. That's where I work!" He said this proudly and stood tall. "I'm a printer's devil!"

Christina noted his ink-rimmed fingernails. "Well, thank you," she said. But what she thought is: *There sure is a lot of eavesdropping going on here...and how did he know Grant was my brother?*

Without another word, the boy slapped his cap back on and pointed in the direction they should travel, then he disappeared down an even narrower lane and slipped out of sight.

Just as Christina and Grant turned to head in the direction of the printer and bookbinder, they were both stopped dead in their tracks when a big, bear paw of a hand slapped both of them on their shoulders.

8 THE COUNTING ROOM

"PAPA!" both kids squealed, as they spun around. Their grandfather gave them a big hug.

"We're so glad to see you!" Christina said.

"Well, I'm glad to see you," said Papa. "Where is everyone else?"

"We're supposed to meet at Uncle Wig's and Aunt Halfpenny's house," said Grant. "Here are the directions!" He did not see his sister shake her head NO and proudly held up the note from Uncle Wig's brother. Or at least that's what he meant to hold up.

Papa took the note and looked puzzled. "These aren't directions. These look like mystery clues to me," he said of the sign images and frowned. "What's up, you two?" he asked, suspicious.

Quickly, Grant swapped notes. "Uh, here are the real directions. The other stuff is just a game Christina and I were playing."

49

Before Papa could protest, Uncle Wig and Aunt Halfpenny, done for the day with their interpreter chores, pranced up hand-in-hand like two big kids in love. Mimi was right behind them, trying to catch up.

In just a minute, Uncle Wig steered them down a dusky lane, beginning to glitter with gas lamps. At the end of the lane, he handed Mimi a key to a perfectly beautiful colonial cottage surrounded by a picket fence covered with late-blooming roses.

To Christina, the gray cedar shakes of the roof looked like fish scales in the lamplight. She watched her grandmother admire the brick of the tall chimney, the wavy glass panes in the windows, and the pretty front door adorned with an autumn wreath.

"Don't tell me this is our abode for the night?" Mimi cried, hugging Aunt Halfpenny.

Christina and Grant were amazed. They were used to staying either in roadside travel motels or fancy skyscraper hotels (depending on where they were) when they traveled with Mimi and Papa on mystery book business. This was like going back to the past to stay in an authentic colonial cottage.

"Wait till you see inside!" chirped Aunt Halfpenny, giving Mimi's shoulders a squeeze.

"Looks like the kind of place where you need extra blankets and might bump your head," Papa said. "Hope there's not a necessary." Uncle Wig laughed, a mischievous twinkle in his eye.

"A necessary what?" Grant asked, as they headed up the walkway.

Christina giggled. She remembered that word from way back in Bath, North Carolina when they'd toured those colonial historic sites. "For what's *necessary*, Grant," she said.

"Ohhh," said Grant, catching on. "You mean like an outhouse—yuck! It's too cold at night for that. I'll just...uh, I'll just..." Flummoxed at just what he would do or not do, he blushed.

"Trust me," said Uncle Wig, coming to the rescue. "This colonial cottage has all the comforts of home."

As Mimi entered the cottage first, and swooned, they all decided that must certainly be true!

Inside the cottage, they all admired the cute rooms filled with old-fashioned comfy furniture of spit-shined wood and overstuffed footstools. A warm fire blazed, logs stacked on coal black andirons, sparks settling on the brick hearth.

"How quaint!" said Mimi.

"C o z y..." muttered Papa, meaning much too small and flowery for him.

Grant and Christina thought it was just perfect, and dashed up the narrow stairs to argue over which room each of them would get.

"Well, we'll leave you to get settled," said Aunt Halfpenny. "I know you've had a long, tiring day. But you still have to eat dinner, so after you freshen up, meet us at Chowning's Tavern for dinner."

Papa looked like he'd prefer to sit by the fire and read *The Virginia Gazette*, even if it was 200-year-ago news. Even Mimi looked

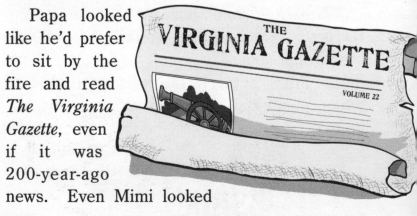

longingly at the stack of books the curator librarian had given her today.

But at the top of the stairs, Christina and Grant (who always overheard any talk of food), cried down: "We'll be there!"

As Uncle Wig and Aunt Halfpenny left, Christina whispered to her brother, "The only things we've learned today about the missing map have been at taverns, so we might as well go to another one."

Grant paid no attention. He had a look of shock on his face.

"Christina!" he said. "We have a disaster on our hands!"

His sister grew pale, thinking maybe her brother had seen a ghost, or worse, a mouse! "What, Grant? What?!"

Her brother spread his arms wide. "Just look around—upstairs and down:

THERE'S NO TELEVISION!"

All the way to Chowning's Tavern, Christina and Grant searched for the Printer and Bookbinder sign.

"You know," Christina said, she and Grant straggling behind their grandparents as they made their way through the darkened village, "this printer clue might be about a map. A map has to be printed."

"Not if it is original," said Grant. "You know, just one, hand-drawn."

Christina stopped in her tracks. "Grant, you're a genius! I never thought of that. What made you think of it?" She wasn't accustomed to being bested by her younger brother.

Grant did a "chicken walk." "Because I'm a GENIUS!" he said. Then he added, "Really, we just learned that in school. You know, about original art versus prints and stuff like that. In art class."

"Hey, you two, catch up!" Papa called back to them. "We're here!"

The two kids scampered to catch up and followed their grandparents into yet another tavern.

Aunt Halfpenny and Uncle Wig were already seated at a large round table. Chowning's was an 18th-century rum and ale-house, but it served icy-cold root beer, which Uncle Wig had already ordered for them all.

Christina and Grant were surprised to see a guest with them. She was a pretty, young woman dressed in a stylish navy blue business suit. A leather portfolio leaned against her chair.

"Meet Ms. Baker," introduced Uncle Wig. "She's a cartographer."

"She fixes cars?" Grant marveled, looking at her outfit and clean nails.

Ms. Baker smiled. "A cartographer is a mapmaker," she explained, making room for Grant and Christina to sit on either side of her.

"Mapmaker?" Christina repeated, trying not to sound too excited.

"Well, really, I'm a map restorer mostly," said Ms. Baker. "We don't have too many cars around Colonial Williamsburg," she said with a wink to Grant, "but we have a lot of old maps that often need to be restored."

"You mean like a librarian?" said Grant. "You keep them all stored so people can find them." The hope in his voice was obvious. Mimi and

Papa looked puzzled. They did not know their grandson could get so excited about old maps.

"Well, more like cleaning and repairing old maps," Ms. Baker said. "Old maps are fragile, and often quite valuable. You can't just spray some cleaner on them. I am trained in how to restore and preserve them without damaging the maps, or altering them in any way."

"Because they are *original?*" asked Grant, determined to play his new GENIUS card every chance he got. Beneath the table, Christina kicked him in the shin and he winced.

Ms. Baker looked impressed. "The ones I work on are," she said with admiration for the young boy's knowledge. "Would you like to come and watch me work tomorrow?" She looked at both children.

Christina and Grant could not contain their joy. Now, Mimi and Papa not only looked confused, they looked just a little suspicious, but they nodded their agreement when Ms. Baker looked their way.

"Well, now that that's decided, let's order!" said Uncle Wig, rubbing his rotund stomach. "Your root beer is sweating, kids, drink up!"

Christina and Grant shared a doomed look. They both despised root beer, which Papa just loved. Still, they both gulped down a big slug, tried not to look sick, and in appreciation for their good manners, Papa poured the rest of their drink into his glass and ordered them a good, old-fashioned colonial lemonade.

As soon as they had ordered (Christina and Grant not too thrilled with the kid's "Half Pint" menu name), a lively program called Gambol's began.

Balladeers cruised the room, playing colonial instruments and singing songs, which they encouraged guests to join in on. Papa, ever the balladeer himself (though mostly of cowboy songs), sang loudly. Christina and Grant rolled their eyes and pretended that they had never seen him before.

Next, old-fashioned games were played, again with the diners' participation. Now this, the kids could get into. When Grant won a game, he gave Christina his "I'm a genius!" look. She stuck her tongue out at him.

Soon, dinner was put down before them. Uncle Wig ate something called Bubble and

Squeak. Papa ate Brunswick Stew. The ladies all ordered Pasties and Peanut Pie. Grant and Christina unbravely ordered good old colonial macaroni and cheese.

As Grant dug into his meal, he sang, "...Put a feather in his cap and call it macaroni!"

With a groan, Christina excused herself and headed to the "necessary," fortunately indoors and quite modern. When returning to the table, she had to pause in front of a small office as a large party of twelve passed by. Much to her surprise, she overheard a suspicious conversation:

"I tell you, the map is worth a fortune!" a deep voice insisted. "And I know exactly where it is. You've just got to trust me on this, Donna."

"Look, John, I've got to finish this billing. You'll get me fired if you don't leave. What you are talking about is dangerous and illegal. Please just leave me alone. And don't bother those kids, either. They are clueless. Please just leave!"

Christina could not see who was speaking for a bank of file cabinets in the way. She took a quick glance up at a sign over the door that said COUNTING ROOM.

What did they say?

She just could not help but wonder if the "kids" referred to were she and Grant. The thought gave her goosebumps and she hurried back to the safety of their table before the man might leave and spot her.

9 NEW FRIENDS

The next morning, Christina and Grant slept in. Their cozy beds with the counterpane quilts were tucked beneath the eaves of the old cottage and the rain pitter-pattered pleasantly just above them.

When they finally went downstairs, they found a housekeeper "dusting up," as she put it. Warm scones had been left for them with butter and cream and strawberry jam. Beside the basket was a note in their grandmother's handwriting:

Off to a meeting...Papa came along...Don't forget Ms. Baker is expecting you. She said to just watch for William and Mary...See you later.
Love,
Mimi

"How do we watch for William and Mary?" Grant asked, chomping into a scone, spewing crumbs which the housekeeper "dusted up" right beneath his nose.

"Why, William and Mary is the college, duckies," she piped up. "Don't know how you watch for it...it's just there—big as stairs! Doubt it's coming to you. Reckon you will have to go to it, duckies. There's slickers and brollys by the door."

"Slickers?" said Grant. "Brollys?" He wondered if that was housekeeper-speak; he had no idea what she meant.

"Raincoats, Grant," said Christina, "and umbrellas."

"Well, why didn't she say so?" Grant grumbled, gobbling down the rest of his scone. "And why does she call us duckies?"

"I think she's English," said Christina, trying on rain slickers until she found a bright yellow one that fit. She grabbed a red umbrella. "Come on, let's go!"

A yellow raincoat fit Grant, more or less. He found a bright blue umbrella.

Christina laughed when she saw him.

"What's so funny?" grumbled her brother, slapping his arms to his sides.

"You do look like a duck!" his sister said.

"Bye, duckies," called the housekeeper from the pantry. "Mind the puddles, now." A hand waved a feather duster from the doorway.

Now Grant was confused. "She wants us to mind the puddles?"

"She means stay clear of them," Christina translated. "Look, here are some rain boots. Let's take these—it's pouring out there."

She tugged on a red pair and Grant found a green pair that fit, more or less. Soon, they stomped out of the cottage and down the steps. Christina hopped across the brick path. Grant stomped hard into each puddle he saw.

"Now that's minding puddles!" he said.

His sister just shook her head, referred to the Colonial Williamsburg map Papa had left for them, and directed her brother toward the college.

Along the way, they spotted men in silk waistcoats and embroidered stockings. Grant was shocked to see a man carrying a needlepoint pocketbook. "Glad I was born in this century!" he said.

Christina tried to explain to her brother how the women wore corsets called *stays* around their ribs and waists, and wooden hoopskirts under their dresses to make them stand out.

"I guess if they lean up against something that hoopskirt pops up and shows their underwear?" asked Grant with a snort.

"Does not!" argued Christina, but secretly she wondered if that could happen.

They passed working folk too, dressed much more simply in rough breeches or simple petticoats. The men nodded and the women curtsied as they passed.

"We think they look funny, but we look like a couple of clowns in this bright rain gear," Christina noted.

"Well don't look now," Grant whispered, "but I think someone is following us!"

Of course Christina immediately whirled around. She saw no one.

"Where?" she asked her brother.

"I don't know," Grant grumbled. "I just FEEL them behind us. Maybe they pop in and out of the shops or behind trees."

"And maybe you ate too much sugar for

breakfast," his sister said, hoping Grant's feelings weren't accurate.

Before she could worry too much about it, the beautiful campus of the College of William and Mary came into view.

"Established 1693!" Grant exclaimed as he stopped to read a historic marker. "Now that's old!"

Suddenly a couple of children splashed up behind them. "Found William and Mary, yet?" they asked Christina and Grant.

The two children turned to see a boy and girl about their ages, only in reverse, also dressed in rain gear, in a matching tartan plaid.

"Uh, yes," Christina said hesitantly, "I believe we have, thank you."

The two kids just grinned at them. "Are you sure?" said the boy.

"Positive?" added the girl.

Grant frowned. "Have you been following us?"

The boy laughed. "As a matter of fact, we have!"

Christina was not amused. "Well, who are you and why are you following us?"

"To help you find William and Mary!" both

kids said in unison,

Now Grant was aggravated. "We just said we found it, thanks very much," he said.

"Positive?" said the boy.

"Are you sure?" said the girl in sing-song teasing voice.

Perplexed, Christina and Grant stared at one another and then the two smarty-pants children. "I think this must be some kind of joke?" she guessed. "So we give up. Tell us the punch line, please."

The boy moaned. "Aw, shucks, we thought you'd figure it out. We've heard you two kids solve mysteries." He thrust his thumb at his chest: "I'm WILLIAM!" he said.

"And I'm MARY!" squeaked his little sister.

"Jo Baker is our aunt," the boy explained. "She told us to meet you and bring you to her office."

"Well, you could have said that right up front," Christina grumbled. But in her heart, she knew that she and Grant would have pulled exactly the same trick exactly the same way.

Soon, the four children scampered through puddles down brick paths across the campus. Along the way, William told them about the famous college.

"Back in the colonial era," he said, "there were few schools and so most folks never learned to read or write. Some became apprentices to learn a skilled trade. But William and Mary had a grammar school, an Indian school, and schools of philosophy and divinity."

"So this college is named after you or you are named after the college?" Grant asked.

William laughed. "The college was named after the king and queen. We are named after our grandparents; it's a family tradition."

"Soooo, your grandparents were King William and Queen Mary?" Grant asked.

"Grant," Christina said, "just keep stomping in the puddles, ok?" And her brother did, stomping in a big one so hard it splashed his sister good!

"We're here!" Mary cried, running up a few steps to a door in a brick building. A small plaque read:

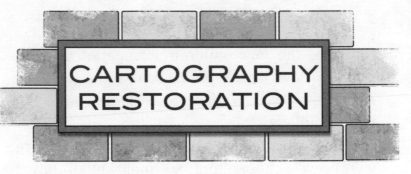

CARTOGRAPHY RESTORATION

Christina shivered. She'd almost forgotten what they were up against—finding a missing map and finding it soon. Eagerly, she went inside as William held the door for her.

Ms. Baker greeted them. She seemed happy to see all the children, but she soon grew somber. "I had just finished restoring the map," she explained.

She took them to a special humidity-controlled lab and showed them the empty table. "It was sitting right here, out of its frame, ready for a final check. I locked up for the night and when I returned the next morning...the map had vanished!" Ms. Baker looked like she might cry.

"There are some rumors that I didn't lock up, that I had an accomplice, or that I even stole the map myself," she said sadly.

"You would never do that!" exclaimed William, looking like he might cry himself. "You love maps!"

His aunt nodded. "I always have," she said earnestly. "Maps don't just tell us where to go, they tell us where we've gone. And this map was so special, being a gift to the queen and all. I'm just devastated and I don't know what to do."

"Just leave it to us!" Grant blurted out.

Ms. Baker looked shocked. "Oh, no!" she said. "Your grandmother told me to remind you kids not to get involved. It could be dangerous. This map is worth a lot of money. We'd better leave the search to the authorities."

Suddenly, Christina caught William's eye. He gave her a serious, but almost imperceptible nod. Christina understood. It was then she knew that she and Grant had two new allies determined to find the map—dangerous or not.

10 A ROTTEN APPLE

Since Ms. Baker had to get back to work, the kids decided to go for a walk around Colonial Williamsburg and see if they could find any clues about where the map might be and who could have stolen it, and why.

Christina quickly caught William and Mary up on the strange clues they had been receiving and the odd conversation she had overheard in the Counting Room at the tavern.

"Sounds like someone's in cahoots with another," William suggested.

"What's cahoots?" ask Grant.

"I mean maybe there is a map stealing ring involved," William explained. "Not just one person, but a group that regularly steals priceless maps, like priceless artwork, and sells it to the highest bidder or fences it on the antique black market."

Christina laughed. "You read too many spy books, maybe?"

Mary said, "That's all my big brother reads! I never know what he's talking about anymore."

"Don't worry about it," William said, grouchily, prancing on ahead. "All we need is a clue."

"Well, I'm the King of Clues!" swore Grant, marching past the others to the front of the group.

"Yeah, sure," said William.

"Uh, no really," Christina said. "He's not kidding. Clues seem to find him more than he finds clues."

As Grant passed them all they could see that what Christina said was true. For there on the back of Grant's pants was another note! Mary ran forward and grabbed it.

"Hey!" shouted Grant. "Leave my bottom alone!"

"Mary's just found the latest clue," Christina told him.

Grant spun around. "But it was on me, so it's mine to read!"

Reluctantly, Mary handed over the orange sticky note.

Grant read aloud:

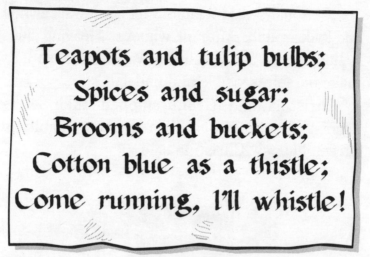

Teapots and tulip bulbs;
Spices and sugar;
Brooms and buckets;
Cotton blue as a thistle;
Come running, I'll whistle!

The other kids just stared at him. The clue made no sense to any of them.

"I think it's a red herring," said William. "It doesn't say anything about the map."

"No," Christina said, "it doesn't. But nothing about this mystery has made much sense so far. What do all those things have in common?"

"You can find them in the shops around here," Mary said.

"Oh, no," said Grant, "not shopping...please don't make me shop!"

"Only till you drop!" teased his sister.

"Seriously," said William, "let's just walk awhile and look around. After all, whoever's leaving clues is finding you, not the other way around, so let's make ourselves visible and findable."

Christina and Grant slapped their arms against their sides. "We're pretty visible in these get-ups!" Christina said.

In the drizzling rain, the four children walked all around the town. They admired the beautiful buildings. Even simple outbuildings, called *dependencies*, were architectural marvels.

The gardens were neat and trimmed. The fallen leaves looked picture-perfect. Everything was so orderly. The quaint shops were neat and tidy.

"That's it!" cried Christina, stopping suddenly in the middle of the street.

"That's what?" asked William.

Christina waved her arms all around. "Everything's just too neat and tidy and orderly here. It's picture-perfect. But there's a rotten apple somewhere. All we have to do is find it."

"As long as it's not in my apple cobbler," said Grant and Mary, giggling.

William looked thoughtful. "So where do you find a rotten apple?" he mused, looking all around. Suddenly, he snapped his fingers. "Come on!" he said, beginning to run. Over his shoulder he called back to the others. "I think I know exactly where to look!"

11 Go to Gaol. Do Not Pass Go. Go Directly to Gaol!

Quickly, the other kids scampered after him, trying to keep up. They stomped through so many puddles that soon they were a muddy mess.

Just as fast as he had stared running, William stopped short in front of a brick building with bars on the window.

"Looks like a jail to me," said Grant.

"It is!" said Mary, with a shiver.

"Oh," said Grant, "more of that weird spelling, hey? If I spelled like that I would be in school spelling test jail," he said. "Or should I say GAY-OL?"

"It's spelled differently, but you still pronounce it jail," William explained.

"Williamsburg was where criminals were tried for any kind of **accusation**. Before they went to court, they were held here. They slept on straw in unheated cells. Some wore leg irons. The food was pretty bad unless the prisoner had money. Sometimes, they were held in **isolation** here for months before their trial date. And many were **condemned**."

"What happened to them then?" Grant asked.

Mary shivered again as her brother said, "If found guilty, they might be fined, lashed, mutilated, or branded. They could even be hung for some offenses. That's what happened to thirteen of Blackbeard's pirates!"

"Uh, I guess that's not what you call the good old days," Grant said, rubbing his neck.

Christina had heard enough. She was wet and cold. "Will, you **digress**. So you think the map thief might be here?" she asked, doubtfully.

William shrugged his shoulders. "I just thought maybe the gaoler might know any news of the map theft and who the suspects might be. He's a friend of Aunt Jo's...and here he comes now!"

What's going on?

From a separate doorway, a man came out and waved at William. "What can I do for you, young Will?" he asked.

"Just wondering," Will replied, "if you've heard anything about the theft of the map my aunt was restoring. You know, the one that's to be presented to the Queen tonight."

Now Christina shivered. So many red herrings. So many clues. So little time, she thought to herself.

Surprisingly, the gaoler grew flustered, his cheeks beaming red as ripe apples. "Well, uh, that is..." he sputtered. "No, Will—don't know a thing. Gotta go, now. Tell your aunt hello for me. Bye, now," he added and hastened off.

The kids looked after him confused.

"What was that all about?" muttered Christina. "I'd say he knew plenty, but wasn't talking."

"Or maybe not allowed to talk?" William speculated. "But clearly something is up, indeed. We just need to figure out what's so **prohibitive** for him to tell us."

"And SOON!" said Christina.

12 INTERESTING INK

Suddenly, Grant began to point and sputter himself. Christina turned, fearing Mimi and Papa had tracked them down and would bring them back to the cottage for the afternoon. And how could they possibly solve this deadline mystery sequestered in a cottage?

"What is it, Grant?" she demanded.

"Look!" said Grant. "It's that design. That thing we've been looking for from the clue." He held up the note for all to see.

"So what?" asked William. "That's just the symbol for the printer and bookbinder."

"What does it mean, Grant?" Mary asked eagerly. It was clear that she thought Grant was a genius at solving mysteries.

"We have no idea!" Christina interrupted. "But let's go check it out, and in a hurry!"

"What's your hurry?" William asked.

Christina pointed down the street. "THAT'S my hurry!" she said, pointing to Mimi and Papa, who had not spied them yet. Fortunately, Mimi dragged Papa into the millinery shop.

"Gotcha!" said William, now understanding. "Let's go!"

The four children tore across the street, dodging other visitors.

To their dismay, when they reached the combination post office, book bindery, and printing office, the clerk was busy with a line of visitors trying to get their postcards back home mailed.

As they waited impatiently, William explained, "You're standing on some pretty historic ground."

"I think it's just soggy ground," Grant mumbled.

"Me, too," Mary said and gave Grant a little smile.

Christina and William exchanged bemused glances then he went on, "This was like the CNN of the colonial era!"

"They had television back then?" asked Grant.

"No, of course not," said William. "But *The Virginia Gazette* was printed here. So were proclamations, posters, and political pamphlets— the kind of writing that changed the world by convincing people that they'd be better off as independent Americans than British subjects."

"Wow!" said Christina, appreciative of what she was hearing. "I can just imagine it was really exciting back then, with all the debate and controversy. Why just look at how heated American presidential elections can get today! Back then, it must have been a powderkeg?"

Just as William was about to agree, the clerk summoned the children forward.

"We just wanted to know if you've heard anything about the missing map for the Queen?" William said.

"If she lost a letter, she'll have to put in a claim," the postmaster said hurriedly, glancing at the line of customers forming behind the children, who obviously had nothing to mail.

Christina giggled. "Thank you, sir," she said. "We'll check with the printer."

William led the way to the print shop where a man in an ink-stained apron operating an ancient press welcomed them. "I'm printing souvenir invitations to the Queen's Ball!" he said proudly. "Would you like to watch?"

"Really," Christina began, "we'd like to know if you've..." She stopped. She'd been about to ask about the map, but realizing how many dead ends she had met, she changed her tact. "I mean, we were just wondering if anyone had asked you for anything unusual lately?"

The busy man looked perplexed. "Like what?" he fished for a hint.

Christina looked around the shop. "Oh, like for special paper, or maybe a print repair kit— you know, like when books are damaged. Or maybe some ink?" She knew she was just guessing in the dark.

But much to their surprise, the printer looked thoughtful and said, "You know, someone did ask me for a certain kind of ink the other day."

"What kind of ink?" asked Mary, eagerly.

Suddenly, the printer reared back and roared with laughter. "Why, 200-year-old ink, of course!" he said, and guffawed again.

The kids just stared at him.

"Thanks," Christina said. "I think that answers our question."

The children turned and left the shop, at yet another dead end. Christina went first, then William, next Grant, and trailing behind came Mary.

Suddenly, Mary grabbed Grant by his coat.

"Hey," Grant grumbled, "why is everyone always grabbing at me?"

Mary looked like her feelings were hurt. "I just wanted to show you this," she said, handing Grant yet another note that had been stuck to the back of his coat.

Grant, who never wanted to hurt anyone's feelings, took the note, "Good job, Mary, thanks!" he said. The little girl beamed.

"What does this one say?" Christina asked, not especially inspired to get another clue that meant nothing.

Grant unfolded the note and read:

"Now that sounds like a threat!" said William.

"Oh, it is!" said Christina with a sigh. She pointed to the familiar handwriting. "That's Mimi's writing. I think she's trying to tell us to get back to the cottage."

"But when did she put that note on Grant's raincoat?" asked William, confused.

"Oh, Mimi has her ways," Grant said, "and eyes in the back of her head!" Mary looked startled.

"We have to obey," Christina said and turned toward the cottage lane. She was surprised when her brother stopped dead in his tracks and began to whistle.

"Grant, what are you doing?" his sister asked, exasperated.

Before Grant could answer, a horse-drawn carriage pulled up and two men in long, black cloaks lifted the children up and into the carriage...and sped off!

13 CARRIAGES AND CONVERSATIONS

The children were shocked! What was happening? They didn't know whether to be scared, if this was a practical joke, or ...

"Hey!" cried Grant. "Who are you, anyway? And why did you grab us?"

"I know you!" Christina exclaimed. "You are George, Uncle Wig's brother! This is not funny! My grandfather is going to be really mad at you—"

Suddenly, Christina recognized the other man in the carriage. "Papa!" she cried. "What's going on?"

Papa gave her a big grin. "Well," he replied, "you know your grandmother wanted you to come home right away, and I figured this was a quick way to pick you up. I asked George here to help me since there are four of you."

"Hello," said George, "I helped Papa locate you kids once we heard Grant whistle." He looked down at Grant. "You've got a good two-fingered whistle there, young man."

"Thanks," Grant replied. "You never know when it will come in handy!"

"Well, we're almost home," Papa remarked as the horse slowed to a trot. And indeed they were stopping in front of the cottage, which with the smoke circling from the chimney and a fall wreath on the door, looked much cheerier than Christina felt.

Papa paid the driver and headed down the sidewalk to the front door, deep in conversation with George. The driver turned his head toward Christina and said, "So, did you have any luck with that map you're looking for?"

Christina stopped in her tracks. Map? How did he know? And why did that voice sound familiar?

"No," she said, frowning. She turned on her heel and walked briskly to the cottage, William and Mary following close behind.

The driver shook his head and pulled the horse's reins, moving the carriage to the curb to let a car pass by.

CLUNK!

Something flew out of the carriage as it sped away. Grant grabbed it. Black ink oozed across his palm. "An ink bottle!" he said softly. As he stood up, he heard the driver speaking on a cell phone. "What do we do now?" he asked. "Do you think we have the original map or not? Those kids don't seem to know anything!"

Grant raced down the sidewalk after the kids. He had to tell them what he had just found—and heard!

14 THE QUEEN IS COMING!

When the kids entered the cottage, they found Mimi sound asleep in front of the fire, clearly worn out. George had left, and Papa was settling down next to Mimi to take a little nap.

Grant ushered the kids into the kitchen. He showed them the ink bottle and relayed the phone conversation he had overheard.

Christina suddenly sat up in her chair. "Now I know where I have heard the driver's voice," she said. "It's the deep voice I heard in the Counting Room!"

"We've got to tell my Aunt Jo Baker," William exclaimed, "so she can call the police!" He grabbed the phone.

RING! RING! RING! RING!

"There's no answer," William said.

"Let me leave a message," Christina said. "I've got a lot to say!"

After Christina finished her phone call, the children trudged up the narrow staircase for a game of checkers in Grant's room. "We might as well do something while we wait to see what happens," Christina remarked. "I hope Ms. Baker gets my message soon!"

For an hour, the house was quiet, the silence broken occasionally by the sound of Papa snoring and a burst of laughter from Grant's room.

At exactly 5:00 p.m., the quiet was broken when Mimi awakened and gave a gigantic roar!

she hollered. "We've overslept! What can we do? Hurry! Hurry!"

"What's going on?" the kids said, rushing down the stairs, even Christina whose hair was mussed from sleeping.

"What's wrong, woman?!" Papa said, waking from his deep sleep like a grumpy bear.

"The, the, the Qu...Qu...Queen is coming!" Mimi screeched. She had jumped up and appeared to be trying to go three places and do five things all at once!"

'WHAT?!" everyone cried at once.

"What Queen?" asked Grant.

"THE QUEEN!" said Mimi, looking frantic, then she slowed down and explained, "It was supposed to be a surprise! The Queen is coming here for high tea before we all go to the ball tonight! And that's almost any minute!"

Instantly, the household went into a frenzy!

Mimi ran up to get dressed, as did Papa. Christina tidied the parlor, and herded the other kids upstairs to get ready. The door knocker clanged and Christina froze, but it was only Uncle Wig and Aunt Halfpenny and others there to set out the tea, flowers, china, and see what else they could do before they slipped out of sight into the kitchen.

Another rap at the door was the official photographer.

Suddenly all was ready! Before anyone could even take a deep breath, the doorknocker was rapped sharply three times. When Papa took a deep breath and opened it, they all spotted a red carpet spread from a beautiful carriage to the doorway.

Almost immediately, a woman alighted from the carriage, a purse over her arm, and made her way down the walkway.

No one breathed as they watched her approach. She came up the few short steps, stopped on the stoop, and gave a big smile. There was no doubt at all—Her Royal Highness, the Queen of England, was at their door!

Just in the nick of time, Papa regained all his gentlemanly decorum and greeted her. "Welcome to our humble abode, Your Royal Highness!" he said gallantly, extending his arm to help her inside.

"Why thank you," she said, taking his arm.

Mimi almost swooned, but quickly snapped to attention and welcomed the Queen inside. "Won't you have a seat here by the fire?" she said.

The children stood like frozen zombies.

THE QUEEN
THE QUEEN
THE QUEEN

was all any of them could think, but they could read Mimi's mind, or at least her face, which appeared to say, "Quit looking like four dunces and bow or curtsy and introduce yourselves!"

Once more, Papa saved the day by making the introductions. One by one he introduced the children, each coming forward and giving a small bow or curtsy, until it was Grant's turn.

Grant, like he always did when he met someone new, just gave a tiny hand wave. "Hi, Queenie," he said pleasantly.

As Mimi almost fainted, Papa gripped her arm. But the Queen just gave a polite chuckle. "You remind me of one of my grandsons when he was your age," she said.

Grant beamed as if that was a true compliment. "Mimi said we were having high tea," he told the Queen, "but I've looked high and low and I have not seen it."

"Grant," Mimi said gently, "high tea just means a formal tea. It's all set on the sideboard as you can see." She waved her arms to the beautiful silver tea service and delightful array of sweets and scones and ripe, red strawberries. The photographer snapped a shot, startling them all with the flash.

Once more, the Queen set them all at ease. "I like any kind of tea, Grant," she said. "But if you prefer a, what do you call it...a PB and J, well that's fine, too."

The children laughed. If the Queen knew peanut butter and jelly, well, she was cool with them. They suddenly felt at ease, which apparently, the Queen was accustomed to making all feel, no matter the circumstances.

"Thanks!" Grant said, and before Christina, who could almost read her brother's mind, could stop him, he added, "And I'm real sorry about your map."

15 THE QUEEN

The Queen looked confused at Grant's remark, but Mimi deflected the comment by announcing, "Tea is served!" Instantly, Uncle Wig and Aunt Halfpenny appeared and began to serve tea as if they did it every day, which really, as part of their interpreter jobs, they actually did.

The children sat straight-backed and well-mannered as the adults talked about travel, the weather, current events, mystery books, writing, grandchildren, and a multitude of other subjects—as if they had known one another forever—until the photographer had snapped a gazillion photos and the tea was cold.

Without even looking at her watch, the Queen announced, "I believe it must be time for us to go to the ball."

She arose as if to leave. Suddenly, she turned and with a twinkle in her eye, she said to the children, "I do believe I am to receive a special gift tonight! Right, Grant?"

The kids froze like statues in a game of tag. They knew she meant the map and they knew that the map had vanished, probably nevermore to be seen.

Grant finally made the first move. "I think it's a surprise!" he warned the Queen. "And we wouldn't want to spoil your surprise, would we?"

Acting all grown up, he headed to the hearth, and to change the subject, he pulled a log from a copper holder and started to stuff it into the roaring fire.

"STOP!"

Christina squealed so loudly that it shocked everyone. She stepped forward and grabbed the log from her brother. In a gasping voice, she said, "Oh, we don't want to put this log on the fire, Grant. We don't want to make Her Royal Highness too warm."

Everyone looked at Christina like she was crazy and she blushed cranberry red. But she'd had no choice. For the log was not a log at all, but a roll of brown paper and on the corner of the paper she had spotted a symbol and an inked fingerprint. This could be the missing map— hidden in plain sight!

Mimi, trying not to appear flustered, helped the Queen to the door and her waiting entourage. "Thank you so much for coming to tea. I'm so thrilled to hear that your grandchildren like my mystery books, especially the one set in London. We will see you soon at the ball!"

Looking slightly miffed and more than a little confused, the Queen gave an odd smile, waved, and departed.

When the door was closed behind her, Papa blared:

"WHAT THE DICKENS IS GOING ON HERE?"

16 WHAT THE DICKENS?

The four children tried to explain all at once about the clues and the men and the strange carriage driver, until Papa blared yet once again:

"HUUUUUSH!"

When it was dead silence, he said, "Christina...explain!"

Christina took the so-called log from her brother. "You know about the missing map," she began. "Well, we've been looking for it." She was afraid to look at her grandmother. "But it's just nowhere to be found. And it's a long story, but we saw this symbol," she said, pointing to the log, "and this ink fingerprint somewhere else. So, it's just possible...."

She stopped talking as she unfurled the "log" and turned the paper over to reveal an old map of the early Virginia colony. "It's just possible," she repeated as they all gasped, "that this IS the map."

Papa took one look and snorted, "This is a fake!" To prove it, he swiped his palm across the map and the drawing smeared, almost as if it had been printed in dust.

Christina said, "Is this the map we've been looking for?" and when William, who had seen the original map with his own eyes nodded, she said, "Then I have this map...or a copy of it...or a fake...in a frame on the wall of my room upstairs!"

Without another word, everyone stormed the narrow staircase and fought their way upstairs. Sure enough, on the wall in her room was the same map.

Papa took it down and took it out of the frame. Once more, he smeared the ink with his hand: "A fake!" he pronounced. "An imposter!"

Now they were all confused. "What is going on?" asked Mary.

"How many maps can there be?" asked William.

I'm so confused!

"Is this some kind of game?" asked Grant.

But Christina asked the real question: "If all these maps are fake—then where's the real one?"

Mimi said nothing, but she had that "I'm using my mystery-solving skills" look in her eye. At last she spoke, "I think I know what's going on, but I'm not sure. Sometimes when you want to hide something, well you hide it in plain sight—like *The Purloined Letter* in Sir Arthur Conan Doyle's famous short story."

"Huh?" said Grant.

"It was a letter hidden, only it was in plain sight right on the desk, so no one thought to pay any attention," Christina explained. "We read that story in book club."

In spite of herself, Mimi laughed. "Very good, Christina," she said. "So if someone was trying to hide the real map, they might distribute *copies* of the map to make it harder for the map thieves to get away with the real one."

"HUH?" Grant repeated.

"The printer!" Christina said softly to herself.

"That's a lot of red herring maps," William said.

"What a ruse," exclaimed Papa. "But how can we prove it?"

Just then, Mimi's cell phone rang. She answered, listened, and nodded. "We'll be right there," she said calmly. Then she turned to the others and said, "Put on your ball clothes. We have to go to the gaol. A map has been...ARRESTED!"

17 AN ARRESTED DEVELOPMENT

"What the Dickens?" said Papa.

"I'll explain when we get there," Mimi said, dashing to her room. "But first, we must get dressed. It's almost time for the Queen's Ball!"

Soon they were all dressed: Papa, handsome in a tuxedo and his cowboy hat...Mimi in a red ball gown...Christina and Mary in pretty white hoopskirt colonial dresses...and William and Grant in breeches, vests, stockings, and belt-buckle shoes. Grant looked miserable.

"I refuse to wear this!" he said. "I look like a girl! And besides, it's all itchy and scratchy."

"Oh, stop grumbling," Mimi said, raking her fingers through Grant's unruly hair. "You look like a proper colonial boy. We all look fine—let's go. There's just no time to waste!"

115

At least it had stopped raining. The clouds parted and a smile of a moon was out with a freckle of a planet nearby. It had warmed up and Papa led them on foot to the gaol.

"What's all this about an arrested map?" he demanded when they got there.

Quite a crowd had gathered. Ms. Baker stood just inside the gaol door. "Come in here!" she said.

When they went inside, they saw on an easel the most beautiful and historic map imaginable. It was clear just looking at it that it was the real thing—not just the original map, but the restored original map. Ms. Baker beamed.

"How did this come about?" asked Mimi, flabbergasted.

"Are you certain it's authentic?" asked Papa, clearly eager to take a test swipe at it.

"Oh, yes!" said Ms. Baker. "I've checked! I spent months restoring this map. It's almost like a child of mine. What a relief to have it back!"

"But back from where?" asked Mimi, "and who stole it?"

Ms. Baker sighed. "There are two men in that cell around the corner who admitted to the crime," she explained. It appears they are part of a gang of professional map thieves who go around the country and steal original historic maps. No one finds out for awhile because they substitute a fake map for the real one. And one reason it's so hard to figure out is that..."

Christina interrupted, "The fake map looks genuine!"

Mimi and Papa looked concerned that their granddaughter would know details about map thievery.

Ms. Baker laughed. "That's right! Because they don't just make any old copy of the original map, they get old paper and old ink, and so it looks absolutely real...if you don't get too close!"

"Like 200-year-old ink?" William guessed.

"Exactly!" said Ms. Baker. "Only this time, there was quite a snafu. Someone else was distributing fake maps too. One fake map can hide the theft, but a lot of fake maps...well, pretty soon, it's clear something's not right."

"Yes," said Papa, "I think we met a couple of those fake maps earlier tonight."

"So...who found the real one?" Mimi asked, with a suspicious look at the children.

Sure enough, Ms. Baker embraced all four kids at once. "These kids!" she exclaimed. They made a visit to the local printer and when they asked about 200-year-old ink, it made someone very nervous. It seems that the thieves could no longer tell their fake maps from the real map! But the printer could tell and he brought the original they had taken to him to make copies and took it somewhere safe."

When everyone looked confused, she added, "To jail! He brought the map here and had it arrested so it would be behind bars for safekeeping until I could come and get it!" And the kids alerted me to call the police to apprehend the suspects!"

"I see," said Mimi. "If there's a mystery afoot, it's hard to keep these kids out of it." She smiled at Grant and Christina and hugged them close. "I'm just glad you are safe!"

"Well," Ms. Baker added, "it's time for the ball and we barely have time to get the map framed and wrapped to give to the Queen!"

"Aw, shucks," said Grant. "Do we still have to go to the silly old Ball? I mean, Queenie is nice and all, but..."

"GRANT!" Mimi said, wagging a red fingernail at her grandson, "If you call that woman Queenie one more time..."

18 THE QUEEN'S BALL

"Quick!" Papa said. "Hurry outdoors and I think I can hail us a carriage and get us there in time. Bring the map!" he said.

Outside, the kids leaned against a big tree that looked at least 200 years old. Grant, fidgety as always, wiggled a loose knot in the trunk. "That was a real 'history mystery,' wasn't it?" he asked.

"Absolutely," Christina replied. "A little confusing, but it all came out clear in the end."

"Well, if we don't get a carriage and we are late, that won't be so good," said William, staring at the empty roadway.

"Aw, Papa, just whistle!" Grant advised his grandfather.

Papa did just that. He let out a loud whistle, and sure enough, from down a side lane appeared a carriage. They hopped inside and dashed to the Governor's Palace, gleaming in the distance.

They arrived just in time to mount the stairs and get in the receiving line before the Queen's carriage appeared, the red carpet was unfurled, and Her Royal Highness, in a beautiful ball gown, diamond tiara glittering, purse over her arm, walked into the Palace.

"Wow!" said Christina, giving Mary's hand a squeeze. "This is one for our diary, isn't it?"

As the welcoming party greeted the Queen and made the formal remarks, Grant and William squirmed in their itchy clothes.

"Be still!" Mimi hissed to them both.

And then the map was presented. The Queen appeared most pleased—after all, all the land that it depicted had once belonged to England.

"I think she's happy!" said Grant.

"I think you're right," Christina said.

"I think we did good, real good," said William.

"I think you're a genius, Grant," Mary said.

Grant beamed. Christina groaned loudly.

"I hope they're not serving any of those red herrings for dinner," said Grant.

19 OH, HISTORY'S A MYSTERY TO ME

The next day, they were all just plumb tuckered out. Fortunately, Mimi and Papa were too tired to even grill Christina and Grant further about the mysterious map mayhem.

"I guess all's well that ends well," was Mimi's only comment. She was much more interested in writing her notes about meeting the Queen while Papa was already heading out to get the *Mystery Girl* ready for their return trip home.

"Mimi," Grant said thoughtfully, munching on leftover scones smothered in strawberry jam. "How come history's so confusing? Do we always know what happened? Are there any mysteries really left?"

"You certainly sound very philosophical this morning, Grant," she said.

"I think he means can we always dot all the i's and cross all the t's," Christina said. "Or sometimes do we just have to wait a long time to see what certain events really meant?"

"Oh, I know what Grant means," said Mimi. "And the answer is that if we weren't there, we can only speculate what really happened in history. You know history was once current events. But the longer time goes by, well, I think there are often many mysteries left behind."

"To be discovered later?" asked Christina.

Mimi stared dreamily into space. "Sometimes, Christina," she said. "And sometimes..." She looked out at the large tree with the loose knothole plug. "Perhaps some things are just made to be mysteries forever. Only time will tell."

POSTLOGUE

It was misty, near icy. The tree roots felt the hoofbeats of the approaching horse long before its rider swerved to a stop, spattering mud on the tree's trunk.

A man, boy really, with flyaway jacket and hair, slid off the saddle and went right to the tree as if they had met before. Hands splayed, he ran his fingers across and down the bark until he found the knothole plug, which he wiggled like a child's loose tooth.

The plug came out easily and his fingers probed the hole. Soon he tugged a ragged piece of parchment from its hiding place. Shielding the note from the spattering rain, he read the faded handwriting carefully, frowned, smiled, and nodded. The family secret was still safe.

Gently, he re-rolled the parchment and tucked it back into the dry socket and stoppered it yet again. Quickly mounting his horse, he galloped off into the rain.

THE END

About the Author

Carole Marsh is an author and publisher who has written many works of fiction and non-fiction for young readers. She travels throughout the United States and around the world to research her books. In 1979 Carole Marsh was named Communicator of the Year for her corporate communications work with major national and international corporations.

Marsh is the founder and CEO of Gallopade International, established in 1979. Today, Gallopade International is widely recognized as a leading source of educational materials for every state and many countries. Marsh and Gallopade were recipients of the 2004 Teachers' Choice Award. Marsh has written more than 50 Carole Marsh Mysteries™. In 2007, she was named Georgia Author of the Year. Years ago, her children, Michele and Michael, were the original characters in her mystery books. Today, they continue the Carole Marsh Books tradition by working at Gallopade. By adding grandchildren Grant and Christina as new mystery characters, she has continued the tradition for a third generation.

Ms. Marsh welcomes correspondence from her readers. You can e-mail her at fanclub@gallopade.com, visit carolemarshmysteries.com, or write to her in care of Gallopade International, P.O. Box 2779, Peachtree City, Georgia, 30269 USA.

Built-In Book Club

Talk About It!

1. If you took a trip to Williamsburg, where would be the first place you would go? What would you want to explore?

2. If you lived in colonial times, what would you have wanted your job to be?

3. Papa, Mimi, Christina and Grant stayed in an old, colonial cottage. Have you ever stayed in or been in an old house? Did you feel like you went back in time?

4. Back in colonial times there were no cars, just horses and carriages! Have you ever ridden a horse or taken a ride on a horse drawn carriage? Would you want a horse to be your only form of transportation?

5. Grant and Christina met the Queen on their mystery adventure. If you could meet anyone from a royal family or anyone famous, who would it be?

6. In colonial times, people dressed very differently. Women wore corsets and men even wore stockings! Would you want to dress in colonial clothes, even for a day?

7. Who was your favorite character in the book? Which character is most like you?

8. What was your favorite part of the book? Why did you like this part?

Built-In Book Club

Bring it to Life!

1. Pretend you are a cartographer. Draw a map of your city or town. Include your school, your house and your favorite places to go. Don't forget to make a legend!

2. Have a colonial party! Find games that were commonly played and play them with your friends. Dress up like you are living in Williamsburg and play the part!

3. Many different foods are mentioned in the mystery. What were some of them? Were there any you didn't recognize? If so, look up what these different dishes are. Do they sound like anything you would eat?

4. Play a game! Split your book club up into two groups. Have each person write down 3 questions from the book. Choose a host to ask the questions to each team. Whoever knows the most about the book wins!

5. Imagine that you are a tradesperson or a shopkeeper in Williamsburg. Create a symbol and a sign for your shop! Keep it simple, colorful and easy to recognize.

Glossary

 accusation: a charge of wrongdoing

docent: a knowledgeable guide

abode: a home

red herring: something intended to divert attention from the real problem

 condemn: to express an unfavorable judgment on

ruse: a trick

curator: the person in charge of a museum

snafu: a badly confused situation

 digress: to wander away from the main topic

 isolation: the complete separation from others

bailiff: an officer employed to make arrests

 prohibitive: serving to forbid something

MATCH THE SIGN WITH THE SHOP
Answers from pages 44 and 45.

 **1**

 **2**

 **3**

 **4**

 **5**

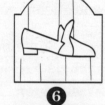 **6**

 7

 **8**

 **9**

 **10**

 11

 12

Williamsburg Trivia

1. Williamsburg is only one of three capitals Virginia has had. The other two? Jamestown and Richmond.

2. Some famous natives of Williamsburg include President George Washington, Martha Washington, Thomas Jefferson, Lawrence Taylor (football player) and Bruce Hornsby (musician).

3. Williamsburg is the home of America's first theater.

4. The College of William and Mary is the second oldest in the United States. Thomas Jefferson went there!

5. Slightly more than half the residents of Williamsburg were black. A few were free, but most were the slaves and servants of the community.

6. Back in colonial times, a person's clothing was a quick clue to their rank in society. Only the privileged never got dirty and wore lace and ruffles.

7. Coffee, chocolate, certain fruits and even sugar were delicacies in Williamsburg! Lump sugar came in the shape of a cone and was kept locked away!

8. Spinning (making yarn or thread) was a common activity for all women. Dyeing and weaving, however, were the work of specialized people and did not take place within a colonial household.

9. In colonial times, the apothecary's shop was like a modern-day drugstore. An apothecary was a pharmacist, a doctor and sometimes even a surgeon!

10. Williamsburg had a printing complex that was the place to go for information. The printing complex included the post office, printing office, and the book bindery. People came there to pick up letters and packages as well as to see the important notices and advertisements that were posted on the walls.

Scavenger Hunt

Want to have some fun? Let's go on a scavenger hunt! See if you can find the items below related to the mystery. (*Teachers: You have permission to reproduce this page for your students.*)

1. ___ The original map of Williamsburg

2. ___ A horse drawn carriage

3. ___ A gourd

4. ___ Duke of Gloucester Street

5. ___ *The Virginia Gazette*

6. ___ The Printer and Bookbinder sign

7. ___ The College of William and Mary

8. ___ The Gaol

9. ___ The Queen

10. ___ Norfolk pottage pyes

Pop Quiz

1. What was the stolen map a map of?

2. Who was the strange judge that ordered the bailiff to take Christina and Grant to The King's Arms?

3. What is the "necessary?"

4. What does a cartographer do for a living?

5. Who do Christina and Grant meet when they are looking for the College of William and Mary?

6. Why did Mimi interrupt the checkers game?

7. What did Christina save from the fire?

8. Where did Christina and Grant finally see the original map?

Enjoy this exciting excerpt from

The Wild Water Mystery of

NIAGARA FALLS

by
Carole Marsh

1 Roll Out the Barrel

"Christina! Look out!" Grant yelled in panic as he watched a massive, wooden barrel rolling straight toward his sister.

But Christina could not hear her brother over the thundering sound of Niagara Falls. Mesmerized, she kept staring through the mist at the mighty rushing water.

Grant lunged for Christina pushing her against a metal railing and out of the barrel's path. She was safe, but Grant was not. Wide eyed, he watched the barrel take aim at him.

Suddenly, a glint of silver flashed in the autumn sunlight. It was a wheelchair and the boy in it was rolling between Grant and the barrel! As the barrel's corner caught the boy's wheel, it popped into the air and jumped off the sidewalk. The wayward barrel raced over the damp grass, collided with a park bench and began to wobble wildly.

Wham!! Splintered wood flew everywhere and a shower of colorful fall leaves rained to the ground as the barrel crashed into a tree.

"Whew!" Grant grabbed his chest in relief as he looked over at his sister.

"Was that barrel headed for me?" Christina asked, confused.

Before Grant could answer, the boy in the wheelchair joined them.

"Are you OK?" he asked.

"I'm sure my ribs will be sore tomorrow," Christina answered, rubbing her side.

"If you hadn't rolled in front of that barrel, I'd be squashed flat as a pancake right now," Grant added.

"Yes, thank you," Christina said as she self-consciously combed her long brown hair with her fingers.

Spinning his wheelchair around, the boy said, "Let's take a look at it!"

As they headed toward the barrel's remains, Christina asked, "Did you see where it came from?"

"No," the boy answered. "That's what so strange about it. When people visit Niagara

Falls, they expect to see a barrel going over the falls, not rolling down the sidewalk."

Grant, who had run ahead, reached the barrel first. "Looks empty!" he shouted.

"Do you think someone was planning to use it to ride over the falls?" Christina asked the boy in the wheelchair.

"Doing any kind of stunt like that is illegal," he answered. "I don't think they'd try it in broad daylight."

"Look at this," Grant said when they joined him beside the barrel. "It looks like some kind of crest," he remarked, tracing the strange mark with his finger.

"One thing's for sure," Christina said, picking up one of the broken boards. "This barrel will never hold anything again."

As Christina turned the board over in her hands, she was surprised to see words written in charcoal.

"What does this mean?" she asked, showing the boys.

JOIN THE RANKS AND ROLL!

"It looks like that barrel did have something inside," Grant exclaimed. "A clue!"

"Grant, don't start..." Christina began to chastise her brother, but something else grabbed her attention. A redheaded man wearing a bright yellow rain coat darted from behind a nearby tree.

"Was he watching us?" Christina wondered.

Her thoughts were interrupted when the boy in the wheelchair spoke. "I don't have a clue what the barrel business is all about, but I'm glad you're both OK. I have to be heading home."

"Wait," Christina said. "You saved my brother's life and I don't even know your name."

"David Hemphill," the boy answered. "I hope you enjoy your visit to Canada!"

WRITE YOUR OWN MYSTERY!

Make up a dramatic title!

You can pick four real kid characters!

Select a real place for the story's setting!

Try writing your first draft!

Edit your first draft!

Read your final draft aloud!

You can add art, photos or illustrations!

Share your book with others and send me a copy!

Six Secret Writing Tips from Carole Marsh!

Non-fiction is factual!

1. Make up good titles – wild and crazy is good!

2. Use strong verbs – action verbs with pizzazz!

3. Edit your work to make it better!

4. Use your own special "voice" to make your work unique!

5. Use a thesaurus and dictionary to find the words that mean what you want to say!

Fiction is made up!

6. Don't worry about rules – use your imagination and have fun!

VISIT THE CAROLE MARSH MYSTERIES WEBSITE

www.carolemarshmysteries.com

- *Check out what's coming up next! Are we coming to your area with our next book release? Maybe you can have your book signed by the author!*

- *Join the Carole Marsh Mysteries Fan Club!*

- *Apply for the chance to be a character in an upcoming Carole Marsh Mystery!*

- *Learn how to write your own mystery!*